Beauty in the Ruins

Simon Stuart

Beauty in the Ruins

Acknowledgements

'piano' was commended and published in
page seventeen Issue 6 (2008)

Thanks to Jane-Marie Mason, Stephen Matthews,
the Melbourne writers Michael de Valle and John
Irving, and to my family and friends.

Beauty in the Ruins
ISBN 978 1 74027 847 8

First published 2014
Reprinted 2016

Ginninderra Press
PO Box 3461 Port Adelaide 5015
www.ginninderrapress.com.au

Contents

For Claudia and Jane

piano

'Princess,' he says having opened his front door.

'Dad.'

My dad has always been more beer gut than man. His blue singlet is pale and frayed around the neck. The tattoo wrapped around his thigh-sized forearm has faded. His short-cropped hair, once dark, is now all but white. He's aged faster than the time that's passed. He's smaller – still huge, though.

'What brings you to town?'

'Remember Gary?'

'Yeah.'

'He's getting married.'

'Well, I'll be.'

Dad worked as a labourer on the railways all his life. His skin is so dark from years out in the weather that he'd almost pass as Aboriginal. I'd never tell him, though; he wouldn't like that.

'Come in,' he says.

The fear of my youth – he wasn't a happy drunk – is turning to pity. He's stooped over as he walks and I follow to the kitchen. It's ten in the morning as I take a seat at the kitchen table. This isn't the house I grew up in. He downsized after Mum died. My brother said, 'It'll give him more drinking money.' At the time I'd thought that was cruel. Then again, he'd been around all those years – I hadn't even made it back for the funeral.

His house is a shit-hole. I'm angry at him. I don't know why. Maybe because this is what he's let himself become? Maybe because he's an arrogant, racist old prick? Maybe because this isn't my home.

'You wanna beer?'

'Bit early for me, Dad.'

'Suit yourself.'

'You have one, though. I'll just have water. '

'I was going to. You wanna tea? Coffee?'

'Tea's fine.' It's safer; God knows what coffee he drinks.

He puts the kettle on. I know about watched kettles. I get up and walk into the living room. The curtains are drawn so I flick on the light switch. It's all our old furniture, seventies stuff. The same photos sit on Mum's piano; I wonder why he bothered keeping it when he moved. I walk to it and lift the lid. The green felt that protects the keys is there; I'd forgotten about it. I think if he calls me Princess again I'll take a swing at him. I remove the felt, pull out the stool and take a seat.

As a kid I'd always mucked around on it. Mum played, not very often; less and less as my brother and I grew up. She probably wasn't very good. She tried to teach me real music from time to time. I wasn't real interested. I was happy making up my own tunes. When I was about twelve she arranged for me to have an official lesson with the only piano teacher in town. My mother was a proud lady; she was always well dressed, so the fact she was wearing her best dress that day was really nothing exceptional. The lesson was to be at eleven a.m.

In the car on the way over, she kept saying, 'Now remember, Stephen: Mrs Manheim.'

'Okay, Mum,' I'd said, getting annoyed. She'd been saying it since she dragged me out of bed that morning.

We arrived early so we had to wait in the car. Mum redid her lipstick in the rear-view mirror.

I immediately took a strong dislike to Mrs Manheim. She was a squat shabby-looking woman.

'Mrs Manheim, thank you for agreeing to teach my son Stephen,' Mum said.

'This is an audition not a lesson.' She had an American accent. Years later, I became a fan of Woody Allen films; she could have been his mother.

'Of course,' Mum said.

She asked me to take a seat at the piano.

I said, 'Thank you, Mrs Manheim.' I played a little Haydn piece that Mum had forced me to learn. I tried my best, not for Mrs Manheim, not for me.

'No, no, no,' she drawled. 'You play like a gypsy.'

'Thank you,' I said.

'Kiddo, it ain't a compliment.' She turned to my mother. 'I won't teach him.'

My mother thanked her for her time.

Driving home, Mum kept telling me how proud she was of me.

I thought, if you're so proud, then why are you crying? I thought it, but even then I knew it wouldn't have been a good thing to say.

After that, I went back to just making up my own songs. Every now and then Mum would just sit and listen.

'How'd ya have ya tea, Princess?' he calls.

I breathe in. I fantasise about going back into the kitchen, walking up to him and smacking him in the head. 'Black's fine,' I call back.

I turn back to the piano and crash my hands into the keyboard. I'm surprised by the anger in the sound. I do it again, moving my fingers even closer together, drowning in the gross, dense brutality I hear. I play. The music has a momentum beyond my ability, beyond my understanding, yet I'm creating it. I'm not playing the happy, wistful or slightly melancholic sounds of my childhood. There is nothing planned or clever here – it is my truth. I'm hearing fear then longing, then the deepest restlessness, anger more anger, then regret, longing, loss.

Silence.

'You remind me of her,' he says from behind me.

'Who?'

'Your mother.'

'Is that why you call me Princess?'

'Nah, mate. She was better than me, smarter.'

I turn. He's sitting in an armchair, his chair. I stand and walk to the coffee table that's between us, stoop and pick up the mug of tea.

'Don't drink that,' he says.

'Why not?'

'It'll be cold.'

I take a sip; it's warm, not hot. 'How long was I playing for?'

'A while, mate. I'll make ya a new one.'

'It's fine.'

'It's no problem,' he says, starting to rise.

'I said leave it.'

'Okay,' he says, settling back into his chair.

I take a seat, the other armchair. Mum's chair.

'How's uni?'

'Not all it's cracked up to be.'

'I remember telling you that.'

'We can't all be labourers, Dad.'

'Watch it.' He stares, nostrils flared.

I stare, heart belting.

I look away.

Silence.

I finish the tea and place the mug on the coffee table. 'I'm going for a smoke,' I say.

'Have it here,' he says, starting to rise again. 'I'll get you an ashtray.'

'No, I'll go out the front. I need the fresh air.'

He smirks.

I step out onto the front porch and the door latches shut behind me. Maybe it's a sign – I'm locked out, I should just keep going.

I don't want a cigarette; I don't want to have to deal with going back inside either. I take a seat on the step.

We've never gotten on. He never hated me; in fact, I know he loves me. We've just always kept each other at a distance. He calls me Princess and I act superior.

I still don't want a cigarette, but light one anyway. I'm sick of cigarettes – I'm sick of the distance and not just with Dad.

He said, 'You remind me of her…smarter, better.' More than that, though, he sat and listened to me play. Maybe he's sick of the distance too? It occurs to me if it wasn't for Gary's wedding I might never have made it back here again. I think of what his life must be like now she's gone, living in this dark little place, drinking beer at ten in the morning.

The door unlatches and opens behind me. I turn.

'Thought you might have shot through,' he says.

'Nah, Dad,' I say, stubbing the cigarette into the step.

'You hungry? I've got some sausages?'

I stand up. I look at him. 'Sounds good, Dad, but no rush, hey.'

'No, no rush.'

'I might have that beer now.'

Boarded up now

'When does she leave?' Carlo asks, standing at ease at the front of the store.

'A month,' I say from behind the register.

'The last time you spoke?'

'Weeks ago.'

'And how long were you together?'

'I don't know. Two, two and half years.' I do know. 'Customer's coming,' I say.

'I will do my rounds.' Carlo heads off to the rear of the store and out onto the back dock. It is from here where he starts his rounds on the hour, every hour. He's done precisely the same for the last three years, every Monday to Thursday six p.m. to midnight.

Carlo returned to the workforce in his late fifties. As far as I can make out, it wasn't by choice. Not that he complains or does a bad job; in fact, quite the opposite. He's always early, his uniform immaculate and, if anything, he takes the job of being a security guard in a small suburban supermarket a little too seriously. He has at least one son that I know of and a daughter who lives overseas. I can't remember him ever missing a shift. In all this time he has only had to use force against a customer once – he's trained.

I've dropped him home a couple of times after work. He lives in a rundown block of units not far from here; this isn't a good area. Carlo rides a bike to work. I've seen him on it from time to time; he looks to be a powerful rider. He told me that he got it out of storage when he landed the security job and that it used to belong to his son.

He said, 'Sometimes I ride as hard as I can, feel the world rush past and sting my face. Then I coast along to catch my breath and take in the scenery.'

I lock the doors and Carlo escorts me to the manager's office. I deposit the night's takings in the safe and sign off the ledger. 'You ready?' I say while extracting my jacket from the back of the chair.

He nods. We move silently through the store. He heads to the main doors while I activate the alarm.

'Well, night,' I say, locking the door from the outside. I start walking away from him towards the car park. From the inner pocket of my jacket I pull out my cigarettes and light one.

'I thought you were stopping the smoking?' he says from behind me.

'I was,' I smile, partly because of his accent and the way he puts his sentences together and partly because we're kind of mates and he's looking out for me.

'Get over this,' he says.

I stop smiling, I stop walking, I turn. 'Pardon?'

'These things, Stephen, left unchecked, they can come to define you.'

I smile again, 'Good night, Carlo.'

'Good night, Stephen.'

I start my car. I'm so angry she's leaving. My mum's not a year dead, but it's a once in a lifetime opportunity. She did ask if I'd go with her, but we both knew that wasn't going to happen. I ease the car out of the parking space. I see Carlo's riding light building speed. I do the same and head straight to a late-night liquor store.

I wake. I feel better than I deserve to. I've drunk every night this week after work; not a new development. I know this lifestyle is both unhealthy and unsustainable, but I can't seem to break the pattern. I'm not going to go into uni today and I'm going to blow off work as well. Over breakfast, which I'm having at two in the afternoon, I decide to head down the street and get a couple of DVDs and something to drink for later.

When I get to work the night after, the fat bald store manager is there.

'Glad you could join us.'

'Craig.'

'The load's coming in late tonight. You're gonna have to stay late and break the back of it, 'cause there's more coming first thing tomorra.'

It's right on six o'clock. Something's missing, different.

'Where's Carlo?' I ask.

'He won't be back. Last night, no sign of trouble, quiet night, nothing doing, he's standing there like a statue, next thing he grabs his chest and drops to the floor. Bloody wonderful. I mean, I pay that security company a fortune and they send me a bloody dinosaur.'

'What?'

'Don't worry. He's not dead or anything.'

'Where is he?'

'How would I know?'

I turn and walk out.

Carlo's unit block really is a dump. Inside his unit is kind of nice, though. Old but expensive furnishings; a huge map of the world hangs on one wall and heaps of framed photos on another. On closer inspection, most of the photos are black and white with younger versions of Carlo staring back from them – all with the same blank expression. He's wearing a military outfit standing to attention in most. One appears to be groomsmen and Carlo on his wedding day. There's no bride in the photo; there aren't many women in any of the photos. Carlo out of uniform, a child on each knee in another; the children are smiling. There is a really old picture with a lone woman; I assume it's of his mother when she was young. It's clear now where he learnt that blank expression.

'It was good of you to come.' Carlo has returned carrying two cups of tea. He's out of coffee.

'You seem all right?'

'I am fine. Mild heart attack, very mild.'

'Glad to hear it. You gave me a bit of a scare.'

'I am fine.'

Silence.

I take a sip from my tea then place the cup back on the saucer. 'Is there anyone who can stay with you?'

'No, I am fine.'

'How about your son?'

'No.'

'Your daughter?'

He smiles and shakes his head.

'Their mother?'

He stares at me, the smile is gone.

'No one?' I stare back.

'No one.' He hasn't blinked.

'Carlo.'

'What?'

I shake my head.

'Drink your tea.'

'Where is everyone?'

'You should be at work, Stephen.'

I look around. 'This place is like…' I look at the wall of photos. 'Where are all those people?'

We fall silent again.

After a time, I say, 'Sorry.'

He smiles. 'I would like you to have something.'

'Carlo, what happened to you?'

'Please accept a gift.'

'What?'

'My bike.'

'Your bike? No.'

'Please.'

'No.'

'I will tell you my story if you accept the bike.'

He's back again with a bottle of port and two glasses; the label says the port is from 1972. He pours two, takes his, holds it to the light, sips, savours it and then begins.

'My ex-wife and I had a favourite restaurant. You have probably been past it. It is down a little laneway in the city. It is closed now. Antonio's Trattoria. This was our special place. We spent some of our happiest times together there, birthdays, anniversaries.'

I smile.

'I got off work one day, I worked late in those days – the job always came first. I knew my wife wouldn't have dinner waiting when I got home. We had been having difficulties. So I thought I would have dinner at my favourite… Anyway, I found myself outside Antonio's Trattoria. I peered through the window. I saw our usual table and my wife was there. My first reaction was joy, then,' he pauses, 'she was not alone. I watched them for some time then I left.'

I say nothing. He refills our ports.

'Antonio's Trattoria is all boarded up now. It is gone. Music groups and theatre companies put their concert posters on those boards. You can still make out Antonio's Trattoria in the faded green writing between those posters.'

'And your wife?'

'I left her.'

'What? Why?'

'She was with him.'

'But they might have just been friends.'

'They were not friends.'

'I don't understand. How could you tell?'

'It was the way she was sitting.'

'What?'

'She was open to him. I am a proud man.' He drained his glass and poured another. 'It is boarded up now. I am not sorry it is gone.'

Carlo had another heart attack within a week, followed by a stroke – a big one. He's in hospital. I've just left; I'm riding his bike. His doctor told me they're going to try and get him into a nursing home. It's a beautiful afternoon. I'm thinking of riding home the long way. I start to pedal harder. I'm flying now, my heart's belting, my lungs feel like they're going to burst. The scenery is flying past; I love the sting of the air on my face. I don't want to end up like old Carlo. I'm gonna call Trish, I'm gonna finish uni, I'm gonna drink less. I'm gonna ride this bike.

The sure

She's a little fatter around the rear. I head to the bar and get a beer. She hasn't seen me. He leans in again to say something. She tips her head back as she laughs. Her shoulders are tanned. She reaches out and touches his arm. She is talking to Joel, a wanker who was sniffing around the whole time we were together. She told me I was wrong about him; they got together shortly after we broke up – I was right. When she left for postgrad studies in Europe, he tagged along. I'd heard, as you do, that he'd come back early.

She sees me. I feel ridiculous in my new clothes as she approaches. She kisses me on the cheek. I can't help but smile.

'Your hair's shorter,' she says.

'So's yours,' I say.

'It's good to see you,' she says.

'It's good to see you.'

She looks away. I look past her to the bar. Our eyes meet again. She smiles, I smile, then my eyes dart to the floor.

'It's a good turn out,' I say.

'Yeah, after being away so long I wasn't sure anyone would remember me.'

'You're pretty hard to forget.'

She smiles.

'Can I get you a drink?' I say the exact moment I notice her full glass.

'You must try this wine,' she says. 'I'll get you one.'

'I can get it. What's it called?'

She waves as if to say 'Don't be silly' and heads to the bar. She returns and we head out into the beer garden. We find a tall table and stand by it. She offers me her open packet of cigarettes. When we were together I smoked, she didn't.

'Thanks.'

Our hands touch as she passes me her lighter. I was so proud I'd given up.

'Kiss me,' she says as I return from the bar.

'Why?' I say, holding out her fresh drink.

'Kiss me,' she says, taking both our drinks and placing them on the table.

I do.

'You're still good,' she says, then bites her bottom lip.

I hope I am. I want her. We talk small. We watch Joel leave.

'He didn't even say goodbye,' she says and turns her head to the right; she always did that when she was sad.

'Sorry,' I say.

All I can see is the sky, but I know I'm in the ocean…

Bubbles pass by my eyes on their way to the surface, I swallow water…

I cough as I take in air, I hear the frantic splash of my arms…

I wake. My heart's belting. She's asleep facing away from me. Today's the first time I've seen or spoken to her since she left for overseas. It's still. I remind myself that I've always been decisive, smart, fearless even.

I slip from her bed and head to the main room of her apartment. The moonlight streams in through the window. From the coffee table I take a cigarette from her packet. I light it with her lighter and sink into her armchair.

I remember when I was about fourteen. My parents, brother and I were having a picnic by the lake. We'd been coming to the same spot for years.

I blow smoke into the moonlight.

There was an island out in that lake. I'd always wanted to swim to it. 'It's today,' I decided while chewing on my sandwich. Later, I ventured into the water, in past my knees, my stomach, I dived, I began to swim.

I stub the cigarette out into her ashtray while exhaling.

About halfway out I stopped swimming and trod water. I could see the island and I could see my parents back on the shore. In the end, I couldn't stay out there any longer. I swam back. It wasn't the last time we had a picnic there. I never made it out to that island.

I rest my head back on the chair and close my eyes. Maybe I should just go back to bed? Maybe I should get my stuff and go? Maybe I should drive back to that lake and swim out to that island? It's only about a nine-hour round trip from here. I chuckle and shake my head. I reach forward to the coffee table and take another cigarette.

Not important any more

Out of bed, walking through the familiar dark – sleep won't come again tonight. This is my pattern. I turn the kitchen light on, an empty bottle of red in the sink.

The smokers are gathered around the big drum filled with fire, laughing, drinking. Some of the boys are hugging some of the girls. Some of the boys are hugging some of the boys. Laughter explodes. One of the men runs to the wood heap. On his return he throws a log in the drum. The fire surges, they all hoot.

I shiver and pull up the collar of my jacket. One of them starts to sing, they all join in. I light a cigarette. It's a mistake, they notice me.

'You must be freezing over there.'

'I'm right.' The words catch in my throat.

Then they all start. 'Join us. C'mon, join us.'

I start walking towards them. I know I'm going to get stuck in a whole lot of shallow conversation. I know I'm going to end up offending someone. I should have been home hours ago. Why does it take so long to organise my money?

I take a seat on my chair by the radiator and flick it on. I feel sick. I pour a port from a bottle that lives by my chair and start reading from a book I've read before; it used to make me happy. I put it down and pick up her letter – She loved me…

'Next.'

'Good evening.'

She ignores me.

Beep, beep, beep, beep.

'Nine dollars and forty cents.'

'And a packet of B&H Special Filters.'

'Nineteen twenty.'

'Thanks,' I say handing her a twenty.

'There you go,' she says as she drops the change into my hand.

The coins spill onto the counter.

'Thanks so much,' I say, staring the rude cow in the eye.

'Next,' she says, looking beyond me.

Home, I turn the ignition off and release the latch for the boot. Out of the car, I pull out my old keyboard and the shopping. I climb the stairs to our flat. As my key goes in the lock, the light inside goes on. Fuck, I'm really late – she's up.

I aim the port bottle at the glass…

'Stop it! You're upsetting me.'

'You can only upset yourself,' I say.

'Listen to me. I'm upset. If you loved me, you'd stop.'

'Stop what?'

'Acting crazy about the slightest thing.'

'Grow up.'

'If you loved me, you'd try.'

'All I'm trying to do is live a happy life. It's all I want for you. It's all I want for me.'

'You're going to end up a bitter, lonely old man.'

'You're right, I probably will. It's sad, made sadder by the fact that you seem intent on making it your life's work.'

'Fuck you.'

'Fuck off.'

She stormed out. I got drunk. She had an accident. I woke with a hangover. She never woke again.

I smoke inside now she's gone – I drink a lot – I don't play the piano or my old keyboard any more. I run my fingers through my beard – I think about that last night…

'What are you doing up?' I ask.

'I missed you,' she says, reaching out to put her arms around my neck.

'Hey, can you just let me get through the door and put this stuff down.'

'You're late.'

'Yeah, there was a party after the show. I got some groceries too.'

'Milk?'

'Yes.'

'We're out.'

'Thought we would be, knew you'd forget to get any.'

'Sorry,' she says as we walk into the kitchen.

'This place looks like a bomb hit it.'

'It's not that bad.'

'You haven't even done the fucking dishes.'

'Stop it! You're upsetting me.'

'You can only upset your…

I stub out my cigarette and pick up her letter again – she loved me.

Falling boy

It occurred to Millie that this was the most eye contact Marcus had made with her in years. As he was talking, his voice was getting higher like it always did when he was excited or stressed. He was using his hands a lot too. This intense Marcus was the one she had fallen in love with. It was the Marcus she had almost forgotten had ever existed.

They had met when she was eighteen and he was twenty-three. He was in his fifth year studying law when she arrived in his country and began attending his university. In time, they moved into his house together. He graduated and got a job in another city. He decided she should come with him. Her family didn't agree that she should drop out of uni and follow him. He said, 'I'm your family now.' She went, she fell pregnant. She lost his baby. Time passed.

Now, in a café, in the middle of a food court in a suburban shopping centre, he thought they had grown apart and that it was time they both moved on with their lives. Millie was twenty-five.

Millie got a job in a department store. She rented a flat. She bought some pot plants and some fabric and made new curtains. She got approval from the real estate agent and repainted her bedroom. The department store reduced her hours from thirty to twenty-four a week, so Millie advertised and got a flatmate to share the expenses.

'I tried to dye it blonde,' Fiona said, having just arrived home with green hair and carrying grocery bags.

Millie smiled then shot her eyes to the ground as her cheeks began to burn.

'Open this,' Fiona said, passing Millie a bottle of white wine that she produced from one of the grocery bags. 'I'm cooking tonight.' Fiona was wearing a black dress with multi-pastel-coloured stockings and lace-up boots.

'Do you have friends coming over?' Millie asked.

'What?'

'I'm sorry.'

'Don't apologise, just speak up.'

'I'm sorry, it's just that if you have friends coming over I can stay in my room.'

'Don't be silly. It's a special dinner for you.'

'Me? Why?'

'Because of everything you do around here. You do all the cleaning, you take care of paying all the bills, we never run out of milk. You're just wonderful!'

'You don't have to make me dinner.'

'Rubbish! Now, get some candles and put on some music and while you're at it, open the wine!' She smiled, then busied herself laying out the ingredients and preparing the cooking utensils.

Millie opened the wine, pouring Fiona a generous glass and herself a small one. She turned the CD player on and pressed Play. Some strange noise burst from the speakers.

Fiona shouted, 'I love this song!'

'You don't have to eat this mush.'

'It's lovely. Thank you so much,' Millie said.

'Rubbish! It's terrible! You don't have to eat it.'

'But I want to.'

'Forget it. I bought chocolate. Let's skip straight to dessert.'

Millie was putting the dishes in the sink and had lit the stove to boil the kettle for tea when Fiona's mobile started ringing.

'Hey, Bel, what you up to?' Fiona said as she stood up and started walking. 'I can't go out, my hair looks ridiculous,' was the last thing Millie heard Fiona say as she shut her bedroom door behind her.

'We're going out!' she announced as she reappeared from her room twenty minutes later adjusting an earring. Millie was sitting; the two cups of tea were sitting on the table.

'Pardon?'

'Come on, we're going for a drink. You can't wear that.'

'No, I won't go, but you go.'

'Damn it,' Fiona said still struggling with the earring, 'I can't just leave you in the middle of our evening.'

'Yes, you can. Please, I'm fine.'

'Are you sure?'

'Yes, you go.'

'Well, only if you're sure. We must do this again. It was fun.'

Millie smiled and took the first sip of her tea; it was still warm enough to drink.

The front door slammed and Fiona was gone. Millie finished her tea then stood and carried the cups to the kitchen. She poured Fiona's down the sink, then started running the hot water for the dishes. When they were done, she turned the lights off in the living room, brushed her teeth and went to bed.

The next morning, Millie, who was traditionally an early riser, lay staring at the ceiling. She couldn't motivate herself to get out of bed. She wondered if it was because of the wine. It was Sunday; she had done the dishes the previous evening. It was the wine, she concluded as she drifted back to sleep.

When she woke Monday morning, she felt drowsy, almost jet-lagged. She had stayed in bed all the previous day, only getting up for soup and toast in the evening. She hadn't been hungry but thought eating something was important. She didn't shower but did brush her teeth. She wasn't due back at work until tomorrow. She couldn't think of a single thing that needed doing. I'll just rest my eyes for a minute and then get up and eat something.

'It's not like you to be late, Millie,' was the first and only thing her supervisor Margaret said to her at work the next morning.

Millie headed to the park across from the shopping centre where, weather permitting, she always had lunch. She took a seat on the same bench, put her lunch box next to her and looked out at the same view. It was a man-made park, with a man-made pond and garden beds in which man had planted trees. The main attraction was a huge, bright multicoloured plastic climbing, sliding and swinging piece of play equipment. It was a popular destination for young children and their mothers. It was a brisk yet sunny autumn day, so the play equipment was getting a good workout. Millie had already decided not to eat the sandwich she had prepared, but she opened the lunch box and took out the bottle of water.

A young blond-haired boy dressed in overalls and a skivvy waddled more than ran across her field of view. He couldn't have been more than three-years old. His face was ablaze with a smile and he seemed to be emitting a chortling kind of sound as he moved towards the play equipment. As he crossed the threshold from grass to wood chips, he stumbled and crashed to the ground. Millie jolted to her feet then stopped. She watched. The boy was still for some time then erupted into tears. Millie frantically looked around; there must have been twenty mothers scattered around the park. Some were dressed like they had just left the gym, others like they were in the middle of housework and others still who would not look out of place on a fashion show catwalk. They were chatting to each other, attending to other children, drinking takeaway lattes. Not one seemed to be rushing to his aid.

She turned back to the boy. He was on his feet now. He had stopped crying and was brushing the dirt from his knees. He looked at Millie, she smiled at him. His face was tear-stained, yet he returned her smile then resumed his waddle towards his brightly coloured plastic target. She watched him play until his mother came and got him. They walked off holding hands.

Millie was still chewing half a sandwich as she put the lunch box quickly back into her locker and walked briskly to her section of the store.

Margaret broke into a smile as she saw her approaching. 'What are you smiling about, Millie?' she asked.

Throwing boulders

1945 – Somewhere in the South Pacific

1

She had read that the sky melted into the sea. It didn't. A rich blue above, a deeper, darker blue below, the line of the horizon clearly visible.

'When was the last time you heard from him?' asked the young Australian serviceman seated next to her.

'Six years ago,' she said, projecting her voice above the hum of the plane's engines.

'That's a long time.'

'I know, but I have to start looking for him somewhere.' She smiled then turned and looked back out the window. 'It's just so beautiful.'

'Trust me, it really isn't when you get to know it.' He had heard people speak of the great actresses having skin like porcelain. She did. Her hair was dark brown and her features delicate. From her accent it was obvious she was British. 'If you want, I'll take you to meet a man who might be able to help you when we land. He's been out here since before the war. Knows everyone, knows everything.'

'That would be wonderful! Is he easy to find?'

'Mr Parker is never hard to find,' he said with a grin.

A speckle of green and aqua came into view through her window.

'Look!' she said.

He smiled. 'That's it, home sweet home.'

The islands grew closer. They varied in size and shape; the majority were tiny and flat, some larger and mountainous.

'It looks like paradise,' she said all but to herself.

Two of the larger islands had huge yellow scars cut into their surfaces. The plane came around and lined one of them up and shortly after the wheels bounced upon it.

Her blouse stuck to her skin, the sweat tingled on her upper lip and threatened to roll down her back, legs and temples.

'Told you it wasn't beautiful,' said the young Australian. The smile was gone as he lifted her suitcase into the back of a military jeep, then briskly limped to the driver's side. 'Jump in.' He drove quickly and had to shout over the engine, 'I have to report to headquarters as soon as I land, but I'll drop you off at the big hotel in town. The French built it, grand old place. Strictly speaking it's not a hotel any more. Well, it will be again now this is all coming to an end. I think, being a lady and all, you'll be able to get a room there. It's where you'll find old Parker too. He runs the place.'

They were driving along behind a big green truck with a canvas canopy on a wide sandy-coloured road. The wind rushing past was hot and stinging. To the left, through the dust, she could see countless rows of big corrugated metal beehive-like sheds built in perfect lines. She looked up at the sky and saw the beautiful blue from the plane and the green of the mountains. Her eyes snapped back to the road as another big canvas-covered truck travelling in the opposite direction sped by. She looked at the Australian; he seemed unruffled.

The jeep pulled into a more established street. Officers, soldiers, nurses and natives walked across the road paying no attention to the vehicle. They pulled up outside the old hotel with its whitewashed facade.

This is rather grand, she thought. She peeled herself from the seat.

He was already out and had placed her luggage off the road.

'You have been so kind.'

'A pleasure, miss. I hope you find him.'

She smiled.

'I really have to report in. I hate to leave you like this. I drink here occasionally myself. I hope our paths cross.'

'As do I.'

2

'What brings a beautiful girl like you out to this bug-infested hell-hole?'

'I'm looking for my brother, Mr Parker. He fled England just before the outbreak of the war. My family and I know he came out here.'

Mr Parker was a large, bulbous-featured Australian. Even from across the table she could smell him or what she assumed was him, musty and wet. His eyes were a little glazed, kindly and yet to stray from hers. She had found him seated at one of the white cane tables at the rear of the hotel that looked out on to the patio and, beyond that, the bay.

'Deserter, hey? Plenty of those came this way 'round that time.' He mopped at his brow with a handkerchief that was the same discoloured white of his shirt.

She persevered. 'I met a young Australian on the plane who said you know everything about these islands. I was hoping you might be able to help me.'

'Young Australian, hey, said I could help? Catch his name?'

'Ah, in truth, it never came up.'

'You caught mine, though.'

'Mr Parker, I'm hoping you may be able to help me.'

'That sounds like business to me, girl. I never do business without a fresh drink.' His eyes left hers for the first time and presently a young American waiter in military dress came over. 'Another gin and tonic for me and one for the lady.'

She started as if to refuse the drink, but he waved his hand.

'It's amazing out here,' she said. 'I believe you've been out here for some time.'

'Since '29.' He brought the handkerchief to his forehead again. 'I've seen some changes.'

'I daresay you have, Mr Parker.'

He smiled and his big eyes twinkled. 'My first job was managing one of the big coconut plantations, the biggest! It was a very different place back then. Before the war, before the Yanks, I mean. It was like the old wild west from books, a real old frontier town. Gunfights, public guillotining.'

She raised an eyebrow.

'True!' he said.

The drinks arrived. 'Cheers!' he said to her and, 'Don't go too far away,' to the waiter.

She raised her glass to him, smiled and then took a sip of the gin. It was cold.

'You like that?'

'Oh yes, Mr Parker. Now, tell me about these islands.' She leant forward and swept a hand through her hair.

'It was a good life. We worked hard, we drank hard, it was paradise. I made a good living, a few deals went my way and I made enough to buy this place in late '37.'

'Oh, you own it?' she said, straightening a little in her chair.

'Yes. Well, I did – rather, I still do. It's just not mine at the moment.'

'I see.'

'I'm sure you don't. As I said, it was a good life here. Then the bloody Japs went and shot up Pearl Harbor. Before anyone knew it, or could do anything about it, the Yanks arrived in early '42. All but overnight they'd cleared landing strips for planes, cut roads, constructed wharfs, hospitals and built those god awful Quonset huts.' He downed the rest of his drink and glared at the bar.

There was a brief commotion behind her, after which the waiter arrived with a fresh drink.

'They raped this island in more ways than one,' Parker said, glaring up at him, 'and if that wasn't bad enough, then our American friends commandeered my hotel for a wartime officers' mess.'

'Will that be all, sir?'

'For now.'

She heard the waiter's footsteps retreating and Parker grinned.

'They're not all bad, my dear. They've poured a heap of money into the island. There's a real economy here now. Since '42, the majority of American troops have come through here for processing before being shipped off to the front. But it's all starting to wind down now. They'll be leaving soon. There are deals to be done. They won't be taking their stuff with 'em, but they aren't gonna be giving it away for free either. They've already started dumping surplus supplies into the sea. I've heard they're gonna bring bulldozers in and flatten the place. They won't be pulling this grand ol' lady down, though.'

He fell silent for a time. 'Would you like another drink?'

'No thank you, Mr Parker.'

'OK. So, this brother of yours, does he have a name?'

She straightened again in her chair. 'George Farrington-Bowles.'

'Doesn't ring a bell.'

A slight panic caught her breath. 'Ah, our family and his friends also called him Jorgi.'

'Crazy Jorgi!' He exploded. 'Jesus, Crazy Jorgi's your brother?'

Sylvia stiffened. 'Well, yes. Well, that is, my brother did go by the name Jorgi.'

'Crazy Jorgi! Now he was a real character,' he laughed. 'A true British gentleman,' he said, putting on his best British accent. He looked away from her. 'He came out here to write poetry if I recall correctly. He had a lot of money, a lot of money. He was my best customer. God, he could drink.'

'Could?' she said.

He turned back to her. 'Yeah, he left back in '42. When the first Yanks arrived, moved out to one of the smaller islands.'

'Do you know which one?'

'Yeah, I know which one.'

'Well? Are you going to tell me?'

'What kind of businessman would I be if I just blurted it out?'

'Oh, I see.'

'Yeah, I think you do.'

'How do I know he's even still alive?'

'He's still my best customer. I just deliver to him these days, for a price of course, a large price. You see, my dear, he wanted his peace and the only way he could guarantee that was by migrating to one of the – how should I put it? – less civilised islands.'

'Name your price, Mr Parker. I'll pay anything. Just tell me which island, and how I can get there.'

'I know you will.' He took a sip from his drink and mopped again at his brow. 'Firstly, though,' he continued, 'you should know that it's still wild out on those islands. The natives here are different, positively civilised by comparison. Out there, the old ways still rule. There are cannibals and all kinds of superstitious rituals and ceremonies that go on. You can't just romp up like you did at my door. You're going to need a plan,' he took another sip, 'and help.'

She nodded.

'I may be able to put you in touch with someone who can escort you. It'll take time, though. Have you got a place to stay?'

'No, not yet.'

He smiled and shook his head. 'You can stay here if you wish, I'll organise you a room.'

'That would be wonderful, Mr Parker, thank you.'

'You'll be needing someone you can trust out here. You strike me as a headstrong young lady. In my experience, headstrong and foolhardy often go hand in hand. We're going to be doing business you and I. You can trust me. I'm an old man now. You have my word you'll be quite safe when you're within these walls. Be careful when you're not.'

'Mr Parker, thank you. I'm putting my immediate future in your hands. As we've established, I have money. Deliver my brother and you can name your price.'

'Sounds like we have a deal, Miss Farrington-Bowles,' he said.

'Please, call me Sylvia.'

'OK, Sylvia.'

'Have you any news for me, Mr Parker?' Sylvia asked the next evening, sitting at the same table as the previous day.

'Miss Sylvia, that is not the way it's done. First things first: was your room to your liking?'

'Oh, very much so, thank you.'

A different waiter in military dress from the day before arrived with two gins and tonic. 'Will you and the lady be dining with us this evening, Mr Parker?'

'Yes, and a third will be joining us at some stage.'

'Very good, sir,' said the waiter and departed.

'Who will be joining us?' she asked.

'All in good time. And how did you spend your day?'

'I rested mainly, though I did go for a walk in the afternoon, but I'm afraid the heat saw an end to that rather quickly.'

'And what were your impressions of my little corner of the Earth?'

'You were right about many things, Mr Parker. The destruction of this beautiful paradise is so sad. The locals are lovely, all smiles and waves. I'm afraid to say, though, that some of the Americans waved and smiled as I walked by too. Not so lovely.'

'Boys will be boys, Miss Sylvia. Well, you're glowing after your day of rest. You look beautiful this evening and a good thing too, for I haven't rested. In fact, I've been rather busy. I think I may have come up with a solution to your problem.'

'Really?' she said, leaning forward. She had expected that he would try and drag this phase out longer.

'I know a man who would be ideal to escort you out to the island. He has done a few – how shall I put it? – sensitive jobs for me in the past. He's a good lad, Australian. We Aussies have to stick together, you know. More significantly, though, he and his boat are well known on these waters. He can come and go as he pleases.'

'Mr Parker, this is wonderful news.'

'He hasn't agreed to it yet. I haven't even told him what it's all about. But I did say I had a business opportunity for him and he's prepared to meet me here tonight. Miss Sylvia, it will be up to you to convince him.'

She smiled at Mr Parker. 'Leave it to me, partner.'

'Partner? Yes, I suppose we are.' He returned the smile. 'There are some things you should know that may make your negotiations a little easier. Wait, here he is. He's early.'

She immediately recognised the man limping slightly towards their table.

'Well, I see you two have met,' he said with a grin. 'Please, don't get up, Mr Parker.'

'I wasn't going to,' Parker said, reaching out his right hand with a broad smile.

Harry shook it then turned to Sylvia. 'Hello. It appears our paths have crossed again after all. My name is Harry Monroe.'

Sylvia stood and offered her right hand. 'It's wonderful to make your acquaintance again, Mr Monroe. Please call me Sylvia.'

He took her hand and shook it gently. 'Please, Harry.'

'Will you join us for dinner?' Parker asked.

'I'd love to, but I have to get back.'

'Please tell me you have time for a drink?'

'I'm afraid not. I was only dropping by to make another time for us to talk. Now that I've officially met your guest, I think I have a pretty good idea what this might be about.'

'Then will you help me, Mr Monroe?'

Harry smiled. 'It's Harry, and I may be able to. Can we meet tomorrow? I have some time off.'

'Of course,' Sylvia replied.

'I'll call on you here in the afternoon, around three. I'll take you out on the water if you like. I can show you the sights and we can talk out there.'

'That sounds wonderful.'

'Wait till you see his boat.'

Sylvia ignored Parker and said, 'I'll be waiting.'

'Until then, Sylvia. Mr Parker.' He nodded and left.

'Small world,' Parker said.

'How do you mean?'

'You having met Harry on the plane and all. I'm assuming your plane departed from Brisbane?'

'Yes.'

'Did he say what he was doing there?'

'I didn't ask.'

'I might get you to do me a little favour and ask him, partner.'

'I'll see what I can do. Why does he limp?'

'There's a bit of a story there. I think it's fair to say he hasn't had a very happy war. He's basically sat it out. A lot of other boys would have happily traded places with him and, if you ask me, he's the luckiest kid out here. He got injured on arrival, broke his leg real bad. Freak accident, fell badly disembarking off the ship, spent months in hospital. Wasn't allowed to go to the front with that leg the way it was.'

'Sounds lucky to me too, Mr Parker.'

'Ah but, you see, he's one of the strange ones. He wanted to fight. He certainly didn't want to go home a cripple who fell down a ramp. So he got a transfer and was working at one of the depots by the wharf. This is back sometime, late '42, maybe early '43. He started coming in here drinking. He's Australian. I took a liking to the boy. Pulled some strings, got him a job taxiing supplies from island to island. So he's spent the last couple of years hopping from one Pacific paradise to another on that strange looking boat of his. He's a good man, Sylvia. He's fair and honourable. I think he'll help you and I think, by helping you, you may be able to help him.'

'How, Mr Parker?'

'The boy came out here looking for adventure. You might yet provide him with one.'

3

'Is this it?' Sylvia asked as they entered what appeared to be a big metal bathtub via its steel-ramped nose.

'It's called a Higgins boat. It started life as a landing craft for our troops. This one never saw the front,' he said while moving to the stern.

'I can see why. Will it float?' she said, inspecting the wooden and metal-plated vessel more closely.

'It was ruled unfit for active duty but, yes, it will float.' He started the engine. It spluttered to life. He grinned and added in a raised voice, 'A bit like me. She got damaged on the way from America and was to be scrapped. It was saved from the gallows and crudely bashed back into shape by some industrious Seabees. Its gun was removed and it was destined to become a party boat. However, the plan was discovered. It was confiscated and re-assigned. She's now an island-hopping courier and delivery vehicle.'

They were bouncing on the small waves as Harry steered them out of the harbour. She looked at him. The wind was blowing his sandy hair in every direction. They were shaded by a crudely constructed awning. He looked towards her and smiled. He was cheeky-looking rather than handsome, but she liked his face.

'I can see you've grown rather fond of this,' she said.

'Yeah, I have. It's been my office for the last two years. It's good to get away from all of that,' he said, gesturing back towards land.

Harry steered a course that hugged the shoreline just beyond the waves. Sylvia held on tight to the side. The boat rocked and she almost lost her grip.

'You should feel what it's like when she's empty,' he said, pointing towards the wooden crates neatly piled and evenly distributed port and starboard. 'Tomorrow's deliveries.'

'Mr Parker tells me you do some sensitive jobs for him.'

'He's big-noting himself, I assure you. Nothing too sinister. I occasionally deliver some unofficial parcels for him, that's all.'

'Like what?'

'Alcohol.'

'I see. He also tells me that you're a terrible fisherman.'

'Why would he say such a horrible thing? He's never seen me fish.'

'He said you stay out all night sometimes and never catch anything.'

'It's funny what people assume. The fact is, I don't stay out on the water all night and I never fish.'

'Why the fishing rod, then?'

'I like helping people along with their assumptions.'

'Really? He said you spend every free moment out on the water fishing.'

'Oh, I bounce out on the waves for a while, that's true, but I don't spend all my time out on the water.'

'Where do you go?'

'You'll see soon enough.'

She spotted the small natural harbour just before Harry turned towards it. He accelerated and drove the boat hard at the beach. She felt the boat touch the bottom and heard the engine stop.

Harry made his way through to the front of the boat and the ramp clanged as it hit the sand. He turned back and said, 'Welcome to my oasis.'

Sylvia stepped out onto the white sand and looked up at the coconut palm trees that circled the little harbour. They provided a shade that reduced the heat and glare to a more manageable level. It was the first time she had been outdoors and hadn't had to shield her eyes since the plane touched down. Beyond a small sand dune she spied a lagoon that was surrounded by hibiscus blooms and other exotic flowers.

She was overtaken by an urge to feel the sand beneath her feet and between her toes, so she went to work unlacing her boots. When she looked up, she saw Harry stripped to his waist, chin up and moving towards the water. She smiled.

The dying sun bounced off the ripple of the waves and momentarily blinded him. A strong breeze gelled his hair back as he waded into the water. He dived; the water passed by him, through him. The relief of feeling less pain in his leg returned, it always did.

Harry had produced some fish and vegetables from the icebox and was cooking them over a small fire. He had introduced her to a new drink – he called it Rocket Fuel in Coconut Milk. It was very good. She had finished her second and was lying back on the beach near him. She closed her eyes and listened to the cicadas and the fire crackle.

'This food is beautiful, Harry.'

He nodded and kept chewing.

'Mr Parker says there are deals to be done out here now.'

'He's right. He usually is. These islands were the nerve centre of the Pacific campaign. This new bomb they've dropped on Japan will either see the Japs surrender or be annihilated. Either way, the Americans will be gone. Parker will do well, you can rest assured of that. It's the rest of civilisation I worry about.'

'He appears to be doing well now. I know he owns that hotel, but he pushes the Americans around like he's running their war effort as well.'

'There is a rumour,' he said putting his plate down on the sand, 'that he blackmailed someone high up in the American ranks. That's how he regained control of his hotel. The story goes that a young native girl was found naked in one of the big brass's bedroom. It's not really a secret, more like common knowledge. A better kept secret is that Parker planted her there.'

'Clever,' she said.

The sky blazed and turned everything red. It bled into the reflection of the ocean. Was it the heat or the Rocket Fuel in Coconut Milk that made the light shimmer slightly and the crisp line of the horizon waver?

She lay on the sand watching him fix himself another drink. 'What did you do before all of this began?' she asked.

He sat down beside her. 'I was a kid when I arrived here. Well, not a kid – I was twenty. I liked playing cricket. I was born and raised in Sydney. My dad manages a bank – he'd just got me a job in his branch.'

'Why didn't you go straight home after you got injured?'

He half laughed. 'I'd barely started there, I hadn't even started here. I guess I didn't want to get into that habit.'

'What habit?'

'Not finishing what I start.' He leant back and reclined on one elbow. 'And I believe in this war – well, in the Pacific part of it anyway. My dad's brother died in France during the first war. I always wondered why he went. I knew about Empire and all, but he was so far from home, on the other side of the world. When the war broke out in Europe, I was too young to go, but some of my friends lied about their age and went. I wasn't going to do that. It never felt like my fight. But when the Japs came blasting down towards Australia,' he looked out over the red sea, 'well, that was different. I wanted to do something, I wanted to be counted.'

She moved a little closer to him.

'And they promised us all an adventure, of course, just like they had my uncle. That was part of it. And here I am, a cripple who never even fired a shot.'

She looked at him. His eyes looked heavy, his words were beginning to slur.

'Where's my adventure?' he continued. 'I'm like everything out here, rotting. The war has raged and I've been stranded here. I'm a glorified water delivery driver, for Christ's sake.'

It was time to move the conversation on. 'What are you going to do now? When it's all over, I mean.'

'I'm not sure. Is anyone?'

She rolled onto her side to face him resting her head on the palm of her hand. 'At home in England, boys are coming home to their families. A lot of boys will never come home. Fathers, mothers, sons and, yes, even daughters and sisters are searching for the lost. It's the not knowing. You may not be a hero, Harry, in your eyes, but you are to your family, you are to your country. At least you did something. Look at my brother Jorgi. He deserted us and I'm out here trying to find him. Your family will be so proud, Harry.'

They lay silent.

'Don't you realise, helping me is your chance for adventure? To make them proud. I can pay you well. Help me find my brother. All those boys are coming home. It's the not knowing. Why should my family be any different?'

He sat up and drained his drink. 'Being out here, watching the likes of Parker and the American top brass, they repel me. Look what the Hitlers and the Churchills and that mad Jap emperor and the whole bloody lot of them have done to us all.' He looked away. 'It's every man for himself in this shit, dog-eat-dog world. I don't need your money, I don't want your money. So why should I help you? Why should I help anybody?'

'What do you want, Harry? You're going to survive this war. You're one of the lucky ones. What do you want?'

'You're a beautiful woman. I have all the money I need out here. There's only one thing you have that I want.'

He turned back to face her. She was staring at him. She slowly rose to her feet. She stood above him, a black silhouette against the red sky. His vision adjusted and he could see her eyes, gazing into his. Her hands reached to her blouse and slowly unbuttoned it. It fell from her shoulder and caught at her elbow. He smiled, she didn't.

4

Her eyes had not left the back of Harry's sweat-soaked shirt for over two hours. He continued to swing the machete with metronomic fury at the vines and branches. He led, she followed, carrying the pack and the rifle. He stumbled over a tree root and almost fell. They said nothing, they kept moving. She was so thirsty.

His shoulders were beginning to slump, the swing of the machete was growing wayward. She too was exhausted, yet they had to keep going; they were in the middle of the jungle.

He wasn't imagining it; there was a cool breeze. Harry changed the direction in which they had been travelling and started heading towards the source of the breeze. It became moist under foot and the foliage thinned out a little.

'It must be a riverbed,' he said more to himself than to her.

They followed it. A worn track materialised in front of them and the going became easier. The track led to a clearing that opened out into a wide, deep blue lagoon that was fed by a waterfall. Harry shuffled to the edge and fell to his knees. With cupped hands he feverishly splashed water up into his face, ran his wet hands over his neck and through his hair. He made no effort to be quiet, she did the same. He slumped backwards, he smiled at her.

They moved away from the clearing and found a spot hidden from view.

She sat down and leant back against a tree. 'You rest,' she said. 'I'll keep watch.'

He lay down and fashioned a pillow out of the pack. He was asleep within moments.

The previous night, they had slept by the lagoon at his oasis and at high tide Harry had steered the boat out of the harbour and headed to this new island. As day broke, they moored the boat at a jetty that was attached to, and serviced, the huge coconut plantation on the island. While the boat was being unloaded by natives, Harry spoke to a tall man in a wide-brimmed hat. Sylvia assumed this man was in charge, as he didn't help with the unloading. The man and Harry were focused on an area high in the mountain that loomed over them. They both pointed, sometimes simultaneously, at the unknown spot. Harry then shook the man's hand and began moving back towards her.

'Are you coming?' he said with his broad grin.

He had thought of everything. Loose-fitting sturdy khakis for her to change into, which she was wearing, a carefully prepared pack containing water flasks, canned food and some first aid essentials.

Harry collected his rifle, the machete and the pack from the boat and they set out through the coconut plantation. They were walking up hill with the towering coconut palms overhead.

Stopping at a slight clearing, he pointed to the jungle-covered mountain ahead. 'Your brother lives up in there somewhere.'

Harry woke at nightfall to a pulse. He lay still, not knowing for the briefest of moments where he was. Through the canopy of trees he could see the sky now burning red. The air had chilled and for once the insects and birds were all but silent. He strained to listen. Was that singing he could hear? He held his breath. The pulse was a drum, the singing more of a chant than a song. There was some kind of ceremony happening. He quietly sat up. Sylvia stirred beside him.

'I thought you were going to stand guard?' he said.

'What?' she said, still groggy with sleep.

The sky flashed white and was almost immediately followed by thunder.

'The wet's coming.'

'What?'

'We need to get moving.'

They quickly and quietly returned to the lagoon, washed rapidly, then moved back into the dense cover and safety of the foliage. They were travelling along a path that led them back up the mountain. After walking for several minutes, it became apparent, from the increasing volume of the drums, they were getting closer to the ceremony.

Harry was a cautious yet inquisitive man by nature. He had heard drunken American troops often speak of the rituals of these islands. According to the stories, certain tribes were cannibals and some of the ceremonies involved the slaughtering of a hundred pigs. He knew danger lay in getting too close. His instincts told him to get the girl as far away from the drums as possible. But they had to keep climbing the mountain. A wave of anxiety swept through him. He didn't know how to proceed; he was still tired and gripped by fear. He stopped walking.

Sylvia came up beside him and paused. 'I can lead for a while.'

She gently took the machete from his hand and kept walking in the direction they had been heading. He followed.

The track had turned to mud. With every step she thought her boot would be swallowed by the ground. It had been raining hard for over an hour, the light was fading, the jungle glowed green and sagged inwards at them.

The drums were getting louder, yet they still sounded some way off. It occurred to Harry that they might pass by the ceremony and avoid it all together. He took solace in the fact that while he could hear the drums, he knew where the natives were.

'Will this rain ever stop?' she asked as they paused to rest.

'It can last a month,' he said.

'What are we going to do?'

He looked at her. He realised it wasn't just rain running down her cheeks. 'We've come here to find your brother and we're not leaving until we have. We have plenty of food and with this rain, water won't be a problem. It's going to be slow going but I think momentum is important. We've covered a lot of ground already. Are you right to continue a little longer?'

'Yes,' she said and smiled.

'I think we should try and avoid coming into contact with the locals. So we might give that ceremony a wide berth. Agreed?'

'Agreed,' she said.

'I'll lead, you let me know the minute you want to stop. We won't go much further. Keep an eye out for a good place to camp for the night.'

They were moving again in the early light. They hadn't been able to find adequate shelter. It was all but impossible to fall asleep when soaked through. It had not let up overnight and was now even heavier, which yesterday she would not have thought possible. The muscles in her legs screamed at her. Harry was leading. She was glad he couldn't see her. She was crying again; she couldn't stop. The rain stung and her heart felt like it was permanently stuck in her throat.

They were on a path. The jungle remained dense around them, but he knew they must be nearing the top now. And then he saw it. It was almost the size of a cow. It grunted; its huge boar teeth were black and it stood facing him right in the middle of the track. He had often wondered how he would react if he ever came face to face with the enemy. He'd always assumed that enemy would be a Jap or a Nazi.

Harry had never fired at a living thing before; he was a city boy. He aimed his rifle. The mammoth pig seemed to comprehend the threat, yet stood defiant. The animal didn't charge and he suspected it wouldn't any time soon. Harry was not going to retreat, though, and had no time for a stalemate. He was tired, he was hungry, he was calm, his mind was clear. He pulled the trigger. The animal let out a roar and a squeal simultaneously and began charging towards him. He fired again. It slumped to the ground. Harry stood still with the rifle raised, his heart pumping faster than it ever had before. He only lowered the rifle when his hands began to shake.

He walked forward not looking down at the beast. As soon as he was beyond it, he turned back and still not looking down, said, 'Are you coming?'

5

The chickens were going about their daily business in the fenced-off area directly in front of the house and appeared oblivious to the downpour. Rain was leaking in through the thatch-roofed veranda. Jorgi had paper and a pencil resting on the table. Water had already dripped onto it through the roof, but the words 'Contact Parker' had not been spoilt. It was almost ten in the morning; he couldn't remember the last time he had sat out here before noon.

He was feeling much better; he would survive the malaria. Six weeks flat on his back had given his body much needed respite; if nothing else, he'd sweated the alcohol out of his system. Today was the first day he could sit up outside. The local woman had helped him to the chair. He poured a large gin from the bottle she had used to entice him out of bed and took a sip. He'd been observing her weight for some time now; he was sure she was pregnant.

Something moved in the trees beyond the garden. His eyes shot to the wall of the jungle to where two sodden figures emerged. The taller one kept moving forward, holding a rifle and favouring one leg. The smaller one held a machete, the wide-brimmed hat obscuring Jorgi's view of the face.

Harry and Sylvia paused before they broke out of the jungle. The rain continued to teem down yet they could clearly make out a thatch-roofed hut at the opposite side of the clearing.

'This must be it,' Harry said. 'You hang back, I'll approach. He's not expecting us. We don't want to spook him.'

The sky was heavy with grey cloud as Harry pushed through into the clearing. He had walked no more than ten paces.

'Come no further, sir!' announced a raspy, feeble voice from the veranda of the hut.

Harry reached both hands to the sky clutching the rifle between them, as a gesture of surrender and peace, and kept moving forward.

'I said come no further, sir!' The voice was a little stronger.

'I wish you no harm, Jorgi. I bring news of your sister.'

'One step closer and I shall fire!'

Harry could see the seated man quite clearly. He couldn't see a gun, but he obeyed the command and stopped.

'Good,' said the man breathlessly. 'Now state your business.'

'I bring news of your sister.'

'You've been misinformed, sir. I have no sister,' Jorgi said, then looked beyond Harry. 'You come no further too!'

Harry turned to see Sylvia approaching.

She removed the hat and kept coming. 'Jorgi, it's me.'

'And who are you?'

'Sylvia.'

'Sylvia! Well, why didn't you say. Come, come.'

They entered the garden via a little gate and walked to the veranda, scattering the chickens in the process. Sylvia stepped onto the porch first and stared at Jorgi. His face was bloated and much of his thick black hair had fallen away. What was left was greasy like his skin. He looked sick. He would have been all but unrecognisable, if not for his eyes; they were watery and a little bloodshot, but they were still his. He smiled at her but there was no warmth.

He turned to Harry. 'And who, sir, are you?'

'Harry Monroe. I've escorted your sister here.' Harry was relieved to be out of the rain. His leg was killing him; he was spent. He noticed the pad with 'Contact Parker' written on it and was wondering how Jorgi and Parker were connected, as another drop of water bounced onto the page. Harry smiled and offered his hand to shake.

Jorgi ignored the hand. 'I have no sister, Mr Monroe. What you have escorted here is my wife.'

There was a brief moment of chaos in Harry's mind, then it hit him.

'Harry, I owe you an explanation,' he heard Sylvia say.

He needed time. He saw the bottle on the table. 'Do you have another glass?'

'Why, of course, where are my manners. Sylvie, be a dear and get our guest a glass.'

'Shut up, Jorgi,' she said.

'Never mind,' said Harry, taking the bottle from the table, bringing it to his lips and drinking. It was gin. He thought, I deliver gin to this island for Parker.

'You look god awful, woman,' Jorgi said, then turned to Harry. 'Be a good man and save me a swallow.'

Harry removed the bottle from his lips and glared at him, then took another drink.

Jorgi turned back to Sylvia. 'What are you doing here?'

None of this was turning out how she'd planned. She thought, I have to be careful; I'm in the middle of nowhere. She looked at Jorgi. His eyes were boring into her, he was almost snarling at her. His beauty was gone. No wonder he had fled, no wonder he hid. She looked at Harry. His head was down and he was slumped against the wall.

'Well, woman? I'm waiting,' Jorgi said.

She felt he was enjoying this. 'You left without a word,' she began. 'You made me a laughing stock.'

'I'd made a laughing stock of you long before I left.'

'You used me, then you discarded me.'

'Young lady, in those days I used and discarded everybody. Hell, I still do. Some men ride horses, others play cards. What amazes me about you, and the rest of humanity for that matter, is that you think you're special. You knew my reputation. Why did you think I'd treat you any differently? What makes you special?'

'But we were special. You always said that I was your love.'

'You stupid girl, there was never a we. There was only ever your father's money. That's all I desired. Never you. I married you for his money, and when my behaviour threatened his life, his respectability, his nobility, he paid me to leave. But may I add, he sat back idly for months while I made a fool of you. He turned a blind eye to that. So I had to change tack. I started making a fool of him, behaving poorly at social events, racking up bad debts at his favourite haunts. The final straw, though, was seducing and bedding the wife of one of his friends. Sylvie, he was only ever out to save himself, never his little girl. Never forget that. In the end, he paid me to leave.'

'Stop! You're lying! Why would you do this to me?'

'Monroe, finish your drink and remove this wretched tart from my land.'

Harry looked up and stared at Jorgi.

'Stop gawking like a monkey and be gone.'

'You should apologise to the lady,' Harry said.

'I'll do no such thing.'

Harry bought the bottle to his lips and drained it. 'You heard me.'

'Get off my land.'

With that, Harry stepped forward, towering over the seated Jorgi, raised his arm that held the empty bottle and crashed it into his face. All at once, the bottle shattered. Jorgi's nose exploded with blood and the chair rocked back, toppling over. Jorgi's feet tangled in the table coming down on top of him as he hit the ground.

Harry looked at Sylvia and said, 'We're leaving.'

She was frozen.

'Then stay. I'm leaving. If you want off this island, know now this is your only chance with me.' He walked down the steps of the veranda and headed back to the jungle.

6

'The second bomb should do it. The Japs will have to surrender now. And you've paid me in full for services rendered. All in all, a good couple of days,' Parker said, sitting behind the desk in his office.

'Well, thank you again, Mr Parker. If that's all, I'll be going,' Sylvia said, starting to rise from the chair.

'Sit, sit. It's bad enough you won't have a drink with me. At least have a chat. I'm an old man. How often do I get to talk to a pretty girl? So tell me, what happened on the island? Did you catch up with that brother of yours?'

'Yes, I caught up with Jorgi.'

'Well? How did it go?'

'I've made my peace with Jorgi, Mr Parker. And now that our business is concluded, I should be going. I couldn't have done it without you. Please know you have my sincere appreciation and gratitude.'

'You don't want to talk about it, that's fine. As it so happens, Jorgi's been in contact with me, placed an order. Said he's had malaria, didn't mention a visit from his sister. Good to see he's on the mend. He is my best customer after all.'

She stood.

'Did you ever find out what Harry was doing in Brisbane?'

'No, sorry, Mr Parker, it never came up.'

'Oh, never mind, Miss Sylvia,' he said. 'I'll find out soon enough. I always do.'

She smiled, turned and began walking out.

'Will you be leaving us soon, Miss Sylvia? My hotel? My island? You're welcome to stay on. Now I know you pay your debts, I can do you a good price.'

She paused at the door. 'I'm not certain of my next move just yet, Mr Parker.'

'Harry?'

'I'm seeing him tonight,' she said. 'He's taking me out fishing on his boat again.' She smiled and then moved off briskly down the corridor.

Harry stoked the fire with a thick branch. The fire surged and he threw it on. 'If you knew he was such a bastard, why did you come all this way?'

Sylvia was sitting cross-legged preparing the vegetables for their dinner. 'I've thought of nothing else since we left his hut,' she said. She stopped what she was doing. 'When I set out from England all those months ago, I thought Jorgi would still be the man I fell in love with, just a little older. And you know what? That's exactly who he was. I'm glad I did it, I'm glad I came. Because I can move forward now. My life was over. Now it feels like it's only just beginning.'

It wasn't hot, but it was a warm night at Harry's oasis. The rains had lasted five days. When they had arrived back at the main island, he had dropped her off at the wharf in the harbour. They had parted on frosty terms but had agreed to meet again a week later and talk.

'The main reason I'm glad, though, is I'm just so happy I met you.'

Harry shook his head. 'Why did you lie to me?'

'I was desperate, Harry. I needed help. You were just another step, the final hurdle. I'd come so far.'

'I was always going to help you, Sylvia. You didn't have to lie to me.'

'Didn't I? How do you think I got out here? I lied and I cheated every step of the way. Harry, I was desperate.'

'Oh, so I wasn't the first on this little trip of yours...'

'How dare you! Don't you dare take the high moral ground with me. You got your price. We bargained, remember?'

'I was drunk and it wasn't a bargain.'

'What was it, then? You certainly made it very clear that was the asking price.'

Harry stood. 'I'm going for a swim.'

'When I saw Parker, he asked me to find out what you were doing in Brisbane.'

He was back from his swim, the fish was cooking on the fire and he was preparing drinks.

'I was organising some money. I've been thinking I might stay on out here. I can buy the boat and maybe a little piece of land.' He looked around. 'I'd love to buy this little piece of land.' He handed her the drink and sat down beside her. 'But don't tell Parker, please. I don't want people knowing my business.'

'I won't tell Parker,' she said. 'Why tell me?'

He looked at her and grinned. 'You're not people.'

'Why stay, Harry? What do you want from life now?'

He took a sip from his drink and looked out over the sea. 'I'm exhausted. Before you say it, I know everyone is. So for now I just want to rest for a while. In time, I want to build real things, stand for real things. We've lived through years of the alternative. Sylvia, I was always going to help you. I'm sorry.'

'I remember when I was a little girl, my sister, brothers and I would go to this pond near our home. We'd spend hours throwing pebbles into that pond. Some would skim, some would sink. They all left ripples. Those pebbles and that pond taught me something, Harry. I've spent my whole life observing and living in the fallout of the ripples caused by the pebbles we throw. I need you to understand something, Harry, or try to at least. When Jorgi left, it was as if he'd thrown a boulder into that pond. I had to find out why. Once I had made the decision to come all the way out here, it was like me throwing a boulder in the pond too. Meeting you was another boulder. Once boulders start getting thrown around, where does it end?'

They fell silent for a time. The sky was turning orange, the sea breeze was blowing like it always did. Sylvia had been in this paradise for little more than a week and she could already feel she was beginning to take it all for granted. It was an uncertain world, an uncertain future, an uncertain now. How quickly we adjust, she thought.

'What do you want, Sylvia? What do you want most in the world?'

She turned to him. He was looking out to sea, the wind was whipping at his hair.

'I think,' she said, 'that this war has made us grow up too fast and that if you find something worth fighting for, believing in, you should fight for it. I found and lost Jorgi, but he led me to you.' She turned to him. 'Harry, the thing I'd like most in the world is us.'

He turned to face her.

'Are we going to be OK?' she asked.

He took another sip from his drink, then placed it on the ground and lay back on the sand. He hurt and not just his leg. He'd swim again soon, but that could wait. For now he just wanted to be still. This life might have taught Sylvia about pebbles and boulders and ponds, but that's not what he had learnt. He'd seen so many young men arrive out here never to return. And the ones that did return weren't the same. It had taught him that in this world, it all ends. He knew life was all just a distraction, it's fleeting for all. Harry knew it was a lesson that, once truly learnt, could not be untaught.

Sylvia lay back next him and reached out with her hand until it found his. Their fingers intertwined.

Eventually he said, 'God, I hope so. You're all I want too.'

She looked up at the sky. There was no line, no horizon, just the vast deep, dark and rich colours of the evening sky, Harry and her and time, stretching on forever.